FALLEN CREST EXTRAS

NYT BESTSELLING AUTHOR
TIJAN

Interior Formatting by Elaine York, Allusion Graphics, LLC/
Publishing & Book Formatting
www.allusiongraphics.com

FALLEN CREST EXTRAS

These were written for a promo tour I did for *Fallen Crest Home's* book reléase. I added a few extra surprises in here as well, but not all of them were posted, so I wanted to make them available for everyone.

This is done as a thank you to the readers.

These were minimally edited, so read at your own risk.

LOGAN'S RANT

"My rant is nice people! Yes, nice people. I see the disbelief on your face and fuck you. You're probably a nice person, well; guess what. I don't like you. I like people who are smart-asses. I like feisty chicks. I like guys who beat the shit out of other people. Yeah. I said that. That's what I like, because you know why? I can be an asshole then, and I'm still the good guy. And you know what's really annoying about nice people? When you're pissed off, and you're having a day where you just literally want to put your fist through someone's face, and then here comes along a nice person. Like they want to make me feel better, and they're being all nice and kind, and saying sweet things to me, but I don't want it. It's an asshole day. I want to be an asshole that day and I can't when these fucking nice little people come around. You want to know what I have to be then? Nice back to them! I can't hit them. I can't be mean to them. Fuck's sakes. I'm going to hell if I rip on a kind person. Yes. So. Go away kind people. Let me be an asshole. Thank you.

That's my rant. Nice people.

Who the fuck needs them?"

Sam's mouth is hanging open.

Logan sees, narrows his eyes. "What? You're not one of those nice people when I'm being an asshole. You don't make me feel better."

"What do I do then?"

"You tell me to stop being an asshole." He pauses. "And then I stop being an asshole."

She snorts. "Your rant made no sense."

He shrugs. "Did to me. I feel better too." He looks at the interviewer. "Thank you."

SAMANTHA'S RANT

"My rant?" She frowns.

Logan rolls his eyes. "Her rant will be when her iPod turns off and she's in the middle of a run."

"It will not be." She thinks about it, still frowning. "Oh! I have a rant." She looks at Logan. "You."

"Me?!" He jerks upright in his seat. "I'm your rant? We're like family now."

"No. It's you because you can be mean sometimes."

Logan's mouth drops open. "Do you know who you're screwing? I talk. Mason fights! He punches. *He's* the mean one." He snorts and gestures to the interviewer. "He doesn't even talk during interviews. No. No way. Tijan said we have to do this shit, so we're here. I talk. I told her my rant. This nice lady is going to ask Mason what his rant is and you know what his answer will be? Nothing. He'll sit there, stare at her, and probably say, 'these questions'." He shakes his head. "No. No way. I'm being nice here. I'm annoying myself. I want to put my own fist through my own head. That's the role I'm doing. No. You get a new rant. You can't pick me. No fucking way."

Sam narrows her eyes at him. "It's still you."

"Wha--"

She cuts him off, "Because all you do is goddamn talk. Your rant is against nice people? Are you kidding me? You're being mean and you know it. Your girlfriend is one of the nicest people I know! And that's why you love her. Because she loves you, even after all the shit you did when she broke up with you."

"She broke up with me!"

"And you couldn't keep your dick out of someone else for at least a few months? Make sure you couldn't get her back? No. You didn't. You screwed around and your *nice* girlfriend still loved you afterwards. She's a goddamn saint compared to you." Sam finishes, then looks at the interviewer. "Next question, please?"

Logan leans forward. "Can I change my rant?"

MASON'S RANT

"My rant?"

The interview nods her head. "Yes. If you had to rant about something, what would it be?"

He's silent.

A few seconds pass.

More time passes.

A full minute has passed.

He says, "These interviews."

The interviewer takes a breath. "And why's that? Can you expand a little?"

He thinks about it.

He's silent.

Another thirty seconds, and then, "No."

Logan's laughing in the background. "Told you!"

Mason only stares at the interviewer.

HEATHER'S RANT

"My rant? Oh my God. I don't think we have enough time. Is there a time limit on these interviews? Do you have to go somewhere else? Because, honey, I could stay forever. I work. A lot. And I study. And this is my break time. And you're here asking me these kind of questions?" She whistles. "You don't know what Pandora box you just opened." She holds up her hand, her fingers spread out. "I have so many things to rant about, but here's just a few of them. My boyfriend." One finger goes down. "My brother." Another finger. "My boyfriend's sister, or no, no, no. How my boyfriend is about his sister. Not his sister. Bren is fine, but how *he* is, that's a whole other issue." A third finger goes off. "I have to work all the time." A fourth. Only one finger left. "And oh yeah, I'm still poor! You met my friends before, right? They're loaded. They don't understand what the poor person has to deal with. No, no. I'm going to love this interview." She pauses, and cocks her head to the side. "You might want to get comfortable. We're going to be here all day."

NATE'S RANT

"Logan."

The interviewer blinks. "Can you explain?"

"Mason." He pauses, then adds, "And Sam. All of them. I want to rant about all of them." He leans forward, resting his elbows on his knees. "Have you met them? I'm sure you did. They usually go first, and it's because they're the stars of this whole operation. Well, I'm sick of it. I want to be the star. When is it my turn? When am I the first to be interviewed? Why didn't you interview me first? Oh. Wait. I know. Because I'm not the star, and they are."

The interviewer doesn't move. She doesn't say anything. She's not sure if she should even be looking at him.

And then, "And you want to know why they're the stars? Because I'll give it to them. They are. Everything surrounds them. Mason is loved. Holy fuck. All the girls want him. And all the same girls want to be friends with Sam. They feel bad for her, but they all love Logan too. And he's got his own group. They're super protective of him, almost to the part where they get bitter because they think he's getting a raw deal. Everything's about Mason. Logan's the runner-up, but you know why that is, right? I mean, it's obvious." He pauses. The interviewer starts to ask, then he says it, "It's because of how gorgeous they are. So that's my rant. How beautiful my friends are. Because holy shit, you've seen 'em. You know. You're probably hot and bothered with me just talking about them right now. Gorgeous. And Mason with his muscles." He whistles, shaking his head. "So goddamn hot. And his green eyes. I've never seen anything like them, but between you and me I don't think he gets enough attention for his eyes, but they're something. Aren't they?

6

Oh yeah. And Logan. Don't even get me started on Logan, with his dark luscious hair, and his chocolatey, milk chocolatey eyes. Oh yeah." He shakes his head, sighing. "Just stunning people. All of them." He nods. "Yeah. That's why they're the stars, and who can really blame anyone? I'm getting affected right now. I should stop. I should get a tan for my book. I gotta look extra good. Yeah. That's a good idea." He stands up and holds up a finger. "This was lovely, but excuse me. I need to book a tanning salon."

MATTEO'S RANT

"I'm supposed to rant about something?"

"Yes. It can be anything."

He thinks about it, frowning. His forehead wrinkles, then he shakes his head. "Nope. We don't do that in my culture. We're all about the love, surfing, fishing, leis. Yeah. We don't do that. We're happy. I didn't even know what that word meant until today." He pauses. "No, that's not true. I learned it when I met Logan. He rants a lot. He could rant for me. Can we do that?" He doesn't wait. He twists around and hollers, "Logan?! Can you do something for me?"

LOGAN'S ADVICE FOR LIFE

He cracks his knuckles, then settles back in his chair and rests an arm over the top of where Sam had been sitting. He peers at the camera, "You guys want advice from me?" He shakes his head, a coy grin tugging at the side of his mouth. "I don't think you guys are ready for this from me. But--" His eyes narrow and he leans forward. A serious expression settles over his face, and he rests his elbows on his knees. "If you say you want it, who am I to make that judgment call, and that's the first set of advice. 1." He raises a finger in the air. "Fart upwind from others. It's not about being polite. Be rude. That's what farts are. Well, they're hilarious, but if you're going to fart, own it. In fact, that's my second piece of advice. Own it. Whatever it is, whoever you are. Just own it. If you're a bitch, embrace being a bitch. People like being genuine. You can be a total asshole and people will still like you if you say you're being an asshole. Don't hide it. Hug it to you. Be the biggest, baddest bitch or asshole you can be. Your life will be a lot easier too. No more being fake. No more trying to hide or avoiding accountability. And third piece of advice: sex. No, really. Sex. Love it. Relish it. Be sexified. Love who you are as a person and love your body. Embracing sex is a big part of that. Don't hide from that either. I mean, why the hell would you? I feel sorry for those people." He looks around. "I feel like I'm the only one being asked questions. Someone else come in here. Jax! Jax--Heather Jax, get over here. You answer some of these questions."

HEATHER JAX'S ADVICE

"You want advice from me? Are you sure?" She looks behind her. "No one else is here, huh?" She thinks a moment, then leans forward and rests her elbows on her knees. Her long dirty-blonde hair falls forward, over her shoulders. "Okay. Well, here's some from me. Work hard. Play hard. And…." Her forehead scrunches up. "Don't date anyone from Roussou. For real. Don't. They have a whole 'crew' system there and if you have a boyfriend who has a sister that goes to school there, yeah. It's going to mess up your love life. Just avoid it at all costs." She looks down to the floor. "Yeah. That's it for me. I guess I'm boring. Why am I here? I usually don't answer these questions." She looks around. "Mark?! Are you here? You could give advice too."

MARK DECRAW'S ADVICE

He sits there, staring at the interviewer.

The interviewer asks, "Do you have any advice to give us?"

"Who is us?" He scratches behind his ear. "Who am I talking to?"

"To us. To me. To….readers who like the series. Give us some advice for life."

"Uh…." He thinks a moment, then holds up a finger. "Get a really good mom like mine. And if you don't have one, find one, like Sam did. She lucked out. She wasn't looking, but she got us. Oh--don't be afraid to do what's best for your loved ones. I spoke up against Mason. I'm going to own that. I don't know. He…I worry about Sam sometimes, but I should. She's my sister. You know? Do you understand? I mean, yeah, they're soulmates. And yeah, Sam doesn't really listen to anyone except Mason and Logan so my opinion doesn't matter, but I'm her brother now. I'm her real stepbrother, well--so are they, but you know what I mean. I was her real stepbrother a whole year before them. That counts, right? I'm not sleeping with her. I don't look at her like that. If anyone, I'm the genuine brother to her. My opinion should matter, but it doesn't. Mason shut me down, literally. I think he actually told me to shut up and sit down. See what I did there? Shut down. Shut up and sit down. Yeah. I put them together. Okay-- more advice. Uh." He cocks his head to the side, his eyes narrowing. He shrugs. "I don't know, maybe just be really sure who you love. Yeah. Get a good mom like I have, if a girl is generally known as a bitch, don't date her because if you fall in love with her, then…. You're stuck with her." He winces. "I hope Cass never sees this. She'll take my nuts. I should stop giving advice." He nods to himself and stands, throwing up a peace sign. "Peace. Love. Prosper. My advice, everyone!"

CASS' (MARK'S BITCH GIRLFRIEND) ADVICE

"I have amazing advice. Only fuck someone rich. Don't fall in love with that fucker, because you have to look out for yourself, and if you do fall in love--just run." She looks to the side and raises her voice. "Yeah, I'm talking about you, Mark. I should follow my own advice and RUN!"

He yells back, "Start running. I'm not stopping you. I'll just sic Sam after you. She'll lap you in seconds."

Cass groans, slumping down in her chair. "That's my other advice. If you fall in love with someone whose mother and stepsister hate you, your life is going to be miserable. My life is going to be miserable." She shudders, but stands and leaves.

The interviewer turns to the camera. "I had more questions for her too."

The camera guy shrugs.

QUESTIONS & ANSWERS

Hamburgers or hot dogs?

Logan scoffs. "Is that even a question? Wait. Are we the hamburger or hotdogs? Are we eating them? What are they being used for?" He thinks a second, then shrugs. "I'm usually always going to go for the wiener, but I'd rather a steak if we're talking about eating. Are we talking about eating?"

Mason shrugs, his arms crossed over his chest. "Between the two, a big hamburger, but I'd go steak too."

Sam shakes her head. "Neither. Sushi for me."

Nate points to Mason and Logan. "Yeah, I'm going with them. Big ass red steak."

Matteo shudders. "You all are wrong. A big pork roast. That's the way to do it."

Heather wrinkles her nose. "I'm usually up for a hamburger, but listening to them is making me want to go vegetarian." She looks at Logan. "Do not tell my brother that. He'll never shut up."

If you had a pet, what would it be?

Sam speaks up first, shooting her hand in the air. "A German Shepherd! Yes. A big running dog."

Mason and Logan are nodding. Mason says, "I'm down with that. A German Shepherd."

Heather shakes her head. "Nope. I want a pet pig. I don't care about the jokes. I don't care about the rules. I am getting a pet pig and that pig is going to work with me every day. He's going to be my companion."

Matteo is watching her. "You know what I just answered the food question with, right?"

She holds up her hand. "I'm not hearing you. I know you're not going to say pig, though."

He laughs, then looks at the interviewer. "I want a big tortoise. Those things can be huge, slow, but awesome pets."

Everyone is looking at him.

He says, "What?"

"A tortoise?" Sam asks.

He shrugs. "Why not? It's whatever we want, right?"

Nate leans forward. "I want a llama."

Logan starts laughing. "I want to hear the reason for this one."

Nate answers, "They're big. They're cute. They're fluffy. I think they spit. I mean, why not a llama? I bet we could house-train one."

If you were an animal?

The whole group is sitting in a circle and Logan points to Mark, "He's a duck."

"What? Why am I a duck?"

"Because you're cute, but you look lost half the time." Logan moves to Cass. "A feral Siamese cat."

Cass starts to protest, then shrugs. "I'll take it."

He moves to Heather. "You're like a mustang. All rough, but gorgeous."

She shrugs. "I'll take that too."

To Nate, "A black bear. You're not as bad as a grizzly, but you're curious enough to get in a lot of trouble. And you can be dangerous." Logan winks. "If you're pissed off enough."

Nate doesn't react.

To Matteo, "You're a dolphin. Or a beluga whale. You're Hawaiian so you're all about the ocean and nature, and you have a good heart."

Matteo frowns. "Isn't there a YouTube clip where a beluga tries to eat a kid at a zoo?"

Logan shrugs. "You get hungry. It happens."

He points to Mason. "Black panther." He nods at him. "Enough said."

Points to Sam. "You're a mustang too, but one of those rare types that lives far in the mountain or something."

She asks, "Is that good?"

Mason murmurs to her, "That's a compliment." He reaches for her hand and laces their fingers together.

Then Logan moves to Taylor, and he beams. "And we have a white Swan in our midsts."

Her cheeks pink. "Logan, not everyone thinks that."

He shrugs, leaning over to kiss her cheek. "I don't care. That's what I think, and I speak for the group. That's my job."

"What about you?" the interviewer asks.

"Me? Oh. I'm like a hot and ripped version of Yogi bear. I'm funny, but piss me off and I'll rip your head off." He winks at her.

High school or college?

Everyone, all at once: "High school."

Logan explains, "You don't know us, but we did so much bad shit in high school. College is all about maturing and thinking about how it can impact our future, but high school," he whistles. "Hell yes to high school. I'd go back." He looks at Sam. "Though, maybe not you."

"Yeah. I'd say college. Life was a lot more stable then."

Heather is nodding. "I'm saying high school too. My college wasn't much. I graduated high school and bam, adulthood for me. High school. All the way."

How did you become so awesome? Is there a limit to your awesomeness? How are you able to have friends that aren't as awesome as you?

Logan puffs up his chest. "I was born into excellence. There's no limit. I piss excellence even. And yeah, I just quoted a movie, but I don't have to know which one it was. That's how excellent I am."

Mason looks at him. "They were asking about your awesomeness."

"That too. I'm so fucking awesome, I'm changing it to excellence. #Imsoexcellentnooneforgetaboutit #theexcellentsexmachine."

If you could be a character on any TV show, who would you be and why?

"Dean Winchester, because he's excellently awesome." Logan winks.

Does Nate like gingers?

Everyone laughs, and then Nate rakes a hand over his face. He leans forward, but is silent. Mason laughs and says to the interviewer, "Funny you should ask. Stay tuned."

Nate shakes his head. "Oh man. Is that already starting?"

Logan claps him on the shoulder. "This will be fun. Just wait. Your turn in the hotseat is coming."

Are they watching and waiting for April the Giraffe to give birth?

Logan snorts. "I *am* April the Giraffe. Ya'll just don't know it." He winks.

Mason... what kind of things make you really laugh?

"Logan. When Sam is drunk. When Nate is drunk. If I get drunk." He stops and thinks. "And football wipe-outs. That shit is hilarious."

Why'd Logan choose bright yellow for his Escalade?

Another snort from Logan. "Are you kidding me? Do you not know my personality? I was channeling Logan Echolls from Veronica Mars? I am secretly a marshmallow." He laughs. "Just kidding. It was the only one left on the lot, and I didn't want to wait to order one. My need for speed was that day, not later."

Guilty pleasure?

Logan raises a hand. "Are we talking guilty sex pleasures? Food pleasures? Can we define this question, please?"

Heather shakes her head. "Answer it in general."

"Then sex it is. Any sex. All day sex. Quickie sex. Doggie sex. Mirror sex. Shower sex. Tied-up and blindfold sex." Logan keeps rambling. "Sex in the morning, afternoon, midnight. Drunk sex. Sex with food. Sex with those undies that you can eat. Anal plugs--" Taylor clamps a hand over his mouth, beet red in the face. "Shut up!"

He laughs, the sound muffled.

She clears her throat, trying to smooth a calming hand through her hair. "Next question please."

If Analise and James hadn't cheated, would your paths have run across each other?

Logan glances over to Mason, as does Sam, and Mason leans forward. His eyebrows knit together and he glances to the floor for a moment. His hands clasp together, and then he shares a look with Sam. "I think… we would've eventually crossed paths."

"You think?" she asks, her voice soft.

He nods. "I do. With all the parties, yeah. You would've caught my eye no matter where we were, to be honest."

Logan snorts. "Helps you were smack in our house, though."

Mason laughs softly. "Yeah. I think that speeded things up, but it would've happened. Eventually."

Sam smiles at him. "That makes me feel better."

Logan snorts. "You might've been dating Quinn. Shit. Mase would've broken that up real quick." He narrows his eyes. "I kinda wish I could've seen that too." He whistles under his breath. "If Quinn hates us now, he would've been plotting our murders with that scenario. Fuck. Do-over, please?"

Nate: If you are given a chance by your parents to act in their movie (Since they are film directors) will you take it? Or start an acting career?

"Uh." His eyes widen. His head moves back a half inch. "Yeah. Maybe. I don't know. I've never thought about it, to be honest." He thinks about it again, his eyebrows pulling together. He begins to nod. "Yeah. I think I would. I'd try my hat at being an actor. I'd probably suck at it, but hey. Try everything once, right?" He grins wickedly. "Logan would be so pissed if I became more famous than him. That kind of makes me want to pursue it, just to fuck with him." His head rises slightly, and his shoulders straighten out. "I'm going to call my parents right now. Thank you for that. That's an awesome idea."

He leaves, pulling his cell phone out of his pocket.

What would be your dream vacation?

"A cabin in the mountains." Sam leans forward, her elbows resting on her knees. A dreamy smile tugs at the corner of her mouth. "All my friends there. My family. The ones I don't like can stay at another cabin, a few miles away. And, lots of running paths. A view so it'd have to be by a lake or a river, or overlooking the ocean or something. Trees. And yeah. A big bonfire pit. And no fighting. Just laughing, and having fun with everyone. That's my dream vacation."

She shares a tender look with Mason.

Logan groans on the other side of his brother. "Seriously? How can I follow that up? I just want a sex dungeon, wherever we're all at." He considers it and nods. "Yeah. And maybe a swing from the ceiling. That'd be perfect. And soundproof walls, in case you wanna really let the scream rip, you know what I mean?" He glances over to Taylor. "Right, baby?"

She sighs. "And that's my tender Romeo right there, everyone."

"Huh?"

Logan: If a little girl asked you to dress up as a unicorn, would you do it?

He nods. "Without a doubt, if the girl were named Taylor. Anyone else, it'd have to be non-sex related."

Brazilian wax?

"Fuck. Yes." Logan is nodding emphatically, then gestures to Nate. "Except Monson. He likes a slight bush."

When going out to eat who usually pays?

No one hesitates. They all point to Mason.

Mason nods. "I do. Logan does if I'm not there."

Logan adds, "And Nate does if I'm not there."

Matteo raises a hand. "I also pick up the check--"

"No, you don't." Logan snorts, shaking his head. "Sam does, if Mason, I, or Nate aren't there."

"How do you know? You're not there."

"Because I know Sam, and I know you, and you're a cheap mother fucker sometimes." He smiles. "But we love our SBC-er."

If as a group you were to have a dinner party and we're told you could invite 3 people from the past or present who would they be and why?

Mason says, "Sam's two siblings that died."

Logan had opened his mouth, but shuts it now. "Fuck. We went sentimental with this one?" He shrugs. "Okay. Yeah. Sam's two siblings."

Sam says, "Nate's little brother."

A wave of silence settles over the group.

Then, a moment later, Nate brushes a hand over his eye. "Thanks, Sam."

Mason says to the interviewer, "Those are our three."

Mason: A five-year-old child asks you if Santa Claus is real…. What do you say?

He shrugs. "I'd just say whatever they feel in their heart is what matters. It's not up to me to make that decision for them."

Logan rolls his eyes. "You didn't think that way when we were kids."

Mason laughs. "You're the one who told me Santa Claus wasn't real."

Logan joins in with his laugh. "I might've been bluffing, trying to figure it out myself."

What are you asking Santa for this year?

Mason nods. "Just general health and wellbeing for everyone."

Logan frowns. "That's boring. I'm asking for handcuffs." He winks at Taylor.

She shakes her head. "I thought we already had some."

He shrugs. "Can you ever have enough?"

Sam is laughing, but holds her hand up. "I'm going to be boring and say the same as Mason."

Mark leans forward. "I'm going to ask for a truce between my girlfriend and mom. They're still fighting."

Cass rolls her eyes. "Aren't you supposed to take my side?"

Logan shoots at her, "You got a ring yet?"

She glowers.

He smirks. "Exactly."

If you could only take 1 person, 1 book, and 1 CD to a deserted island, who and what would it be?

Mason shrugs. "I'd take Sam."

"Hey!"

He adds, "You'd take Taylor and you know it."

"Still. I have to protest under the banner of protesting. It's my right."

The interviewer asks Mason, "And a book? A CD?"

He shrugs. "I'd probably take a journal instead of a real book, and maybe...some Otis Taylor."

Logan jerks forward. "I'm taking Taylor, Fifty Shades of Grey, and Beyonce's last album."

Taylor raises her eyebrows. "Beyonce?"

"I've always liked Lemonade." He winks at her.

She sighs, then answers, "I would take Logan, the first Harry Potter book, and I'm going to mix it up with Adele's 21 album."

Mark yelps, shooting a fist in the air. "Yeah! Fire to the Rain!"

Sam laughs. "I'd take Mason. The last JD Robb novel, and I'd take the last Avicii album."

The interviewer turns to Mark.

"Oh!" Mark leans forward. "Yes. I'd take," he frowns. "Shit. Yeah. I'd take Cass--"

"Took long enough to answer that."

He ignores her. "--and I would take the second Harry Potter book, and also Adele's 21 album."

The interviewer looks at Cass.

Logan waves an arm. "Does she even matter? Really?"

"You're an asshole."

He laughs. "I have something to say, but out of respect to Mark, I'm actually keeping quiet. For once."

Bungee jumping or skydiving?

"Skydiving, hell yes." Logan looks to Mason, who nods.

Mason adds, "For sure." He grins at the interviewer. "We've already done bungee jumping."

"And it was awesome, but bring on the fake flying! Fuck yes. It's time to soar. Right, Sam? Right?"

She frowns at him. "No. Not this time. No fake flying for either of you. You can bungee jump, but that's it. I'm not risking losing either of you. Shit." She shudders. "We've been over this, haven't we?"

Taylor speaks, her voice firm, "I agree with Sam. No flying." She locks eyes with Logan. "Unless it's in the bedroom, you ain't going nowhere, buddy."

He groans, then grins. "I'm kind of turned on right now."

Mason what would you give Sam on Valentine's Day?

He doesn't think. He answers right away, "We'd go to my mom's villa in France. I'd hire a masseuse. A private chef. She'd have any alcohol she wanted…" He trails off and looks at her. "You'd probably want to go on a long run that day, right?"

She nods, beaming. "Is that okay?"

He sighs. "I'd have to go with you."

She nods again. "On Valentine's Day? You bet." She leans over and kisses his cheek. "But we could enjoy the pool at your mom's villa."

Sam: Which would be harder for you to give up: coffee or running?

"Running."

Logan laughs. "She tried giving up coffee, and that only made her run more." He snorts. "Figure out the irony there."

Sam shrugs. "Running."

Logan: What do you want your tombstone to say?

"He partied hard. He lived hard. He sexed hard. Now he's going to haunt hard." He winks.

Who would Sam snog, marry or avoid out of Brandon, Channing, or Jackson?

"Snog Brandon, though that makes me uncomfortable saying. I'd avoid Channing, because he's Heather's."

She grins at Heather, who mutters under her breath, "Damn straight. I love my girl."

Sam finishes, "And I'd marry Jackson." She turns to Mason. "I'm sorry."

And out of Quinn, Logan, or Nate?

"Avoid Quinn!" She groans. "I can't answer. They're both family to me. I just can't. I plead the 5th!"

Logan says, "I'd snog and marry Nate."

"Thank you, Logan. I appreciate that."

"Anytime, my husband." He winks.

How much did Analise know about Samantha having horrible friends?

"She totally knew!" Logan bursts out. "I don't care what Sam might say. Analise totally fucking knew, and that made her even worse."

Mason nods.

Everyone is nodding.

Sam just says, "Yeah…"

For Logan. If you could be Mason, Nate, or Sam for a day who would you be?

"I would be Sam for a day when she's hanging out with the girls. One, I'd like to see what it's like to run a freaking marathon and two, I think the girls have a lot of fun. I think they hide it from us sometimes." He looks at Sam, then Heather. "Right? Taylor always looks like she had really great sex every morning after a night out with you guys. What do you all do?"

Taylor barks out a laugh. "Not sex! Logan! That's cheating."

He shrugs. "I still want to know. You have this glow. I'm jealous of it. So yeah." He nods to the interviewer. "I pick Sam, but no screwing my brother. She can't see Mason that day. Or me. I have to be annoying sometimes."

ALTERNATE
BEGINNINGS

AN ALTERNATE BEGINNING THAT WAS CUT

"We've set the date! We're getting married this June."

This was an announcement that should've been received with smiles, cheer, congratulations, the usual merriment. As my mother proclaimed her news over the dinner table, none of that happened. Silence. Pure, awkward, and dread-filled silence filled the room. No one said a thing and for that, I was grateful. Mason sat beside me. Logan was across from me. Mark. Malinda. David. And James. We were all here. The two families, and Analise had thrown that out. She was beaming. Her smile spread from ear to ear, and for a second, my usual loathing for her lessened. She truly was happy. Everyone was waiting for me. I was her daughter. Mason and Logan would follow me in whatever direction I wanted to go, if I wanted to be happy or sarcastic, and I sat there, utterly having no idea how to react.

Malinda cleared her throat. She leaned forward, a timid smile on her face. "Well, congratulate--"

"Fuck this."

All eyes went to Logan, whose lips were twisted in a glare. His eyes locked on his dad's and he leaned forward, his hands holding onto the table like he was keeping himself in his chair. "Are you kidding us?"

James's eyebrow knitted together. "I don't know why you're responding like this. She's been home for a year now. What were you expecting?"

"Maybe to let us know privately."

Mason spoke up and his voice was low, but it pulled everyone's attention. His eyes were locked on their father as well. He wore a mask, not showing his emotion, but a shiver went down my spine nonetheless, even though I had no reason to be scared. I loved Mason. He was my soulmate and Logan was family. The three of us, brought together because of my mother and their father, had become our own unit. We depended on each other when we couldn't rely on anyone else. Since then, David had come back into my life, my father, and with him came Malinda. They were now married and defined what the word 'parent' was to me. When I came home from college, I stayed with them. Mark was Malinda's son and he was family as well, but nothing and no one came as close to Mason and Logan did to me.

"And when would that be?" James glared at his eldest son. "The two of you won't step foot in the house. You're home on holiday this year and you still won't accept any of my calls. Thank God for Malinda, for throwing this dinner or we wouldn't have seen either of our children this holiday. You've all been avoiding us the entire year since Analise returned to Fallen Crest."

Logan snorted. "Don't blame us for wanting to avoid the loony bin reject."

Analise sucked in her breath.

"Logan!" Malinda flashed him a dark look.

He shrugged. "I call it how I see it. Forget this shit." He stood up, nodded to Malinda. "Thanks for the dinner, but I'm out. I got a girlfriend I'd rather spend time with than hear this bullshit."

He left, letting the door shut loudly behind him. He didn't slam it, and that was a testament to Taylor and the effect his girlfriend had on him. PreTaylor Logan would've stuck around, throw a few more barbed taunts at Analise, and then stalked out, slamming the door behind him. Or he would've just started drinking at the dinner table. This Logan left, only a few insults thrown out, and the door didn't slam behind him.

He was maturing.

Mason glanced to me. "What do you want to do?"

And that was the crux of everything. What did I want? I wanted Analise to go away. She'd hurt me enough, but she had played nice for an entire year. She only forced her presence on me a couple times, but I was a sophomore in college. Mason was a junior. Logan was a sophomore with me. We weren't in high school, and holy shit—did that suck. I felt like I had to be mature as well.

I closed my eyes for a moment, just one moment that I wished could've lasted into a thousand moments. When I opened them, Analise was waiting. I let myself study her. She was so beautiful. Her black hair was swept up into a braid that led to a bun. There were no glamorous necklaces, earrings, bracelets, or rings. She would've been dripping in them before she left for the hospital. Instead, everything was bare. She only had a minimal of make-up on her face and she was dressed in a simple red dress. She looked absolutely breathtaking and in that brief moment, she reminded me of the mom I once had. The one when there were good times, not the bad times, not when she was hurting me or scheming to hurt someone else.

Pain flashed in her eyes as she held my gaze. I didn't know if that was genuine, or an act, but it worked. I felt my wall melting, just a tiny bit, and I sighed. "I think we've had dessert. I don't think it'd be rude to leave."

Her eyes shimmered with tears, but she looked down at her lap.

I said, my throat so damn hoarse, "But congratulations Analise." I nodded at James. "You too. You both love each other and have gone through a lot for each other. I've no doubt the wedding will be amazing."

Her head lifted. Her eyes were brimming with unshed tears, and one fell down. She wiped it away, her hand moving gracefully, but she was beaming at me. A small smile tugged at the corners of her mouth. She said, so softly, "Thank you, Samantha."

I nodded, glancing to Malinda. "Do you mind if we leave?"

My stepmother waved at my plate. "Have at it. You came. You ate. You were gracious. Can't be more proud of you, honey."

"Mom, Cass called me before. Can she—"

Mark spoke up as Malinda was talking to me and without missing a beat, her hand went from gesturing to my empty plate to pointing a finger in her son's face. "You might think it's a good time to ask if your girlfriend can spend the night, but believe me, son that I worship, that girl is definitely not welcomed to spend the night."

"Mom." His tone was curt. "Mason sleeps over all the time."

"And that was the deal worked out ahead of time between Mason, Sam, and your stepfather. There's no such deal with your girlfriend." Her hand fell on top of his hand and she squeezed it gently. Her tone softened. "I'm sorry, Marcus. I know it seems hypocritical of me, but you're still my boy. And I'm still not a fan of hers. This is protective-mother coming out. I want to keep my boy as much to myself as possible."

"I'm a sophomore in college, Mom."

"I know." Her voice grew husky. "Trust me, I'm aware."

David leaned forward. As Malinda withdrew her hand and sat back in her chair, automatically leaning closer to her husband, his hand came overs hers. "Maybe Cass can come over tomorrow for dinner?"

Mark sighed, but said, "Yeah. That sounds good." He glanced to me. "Are you coming?"

"I...." ....had no idea. Feeling like a deer caught in headlights, I turned to Mason, who narrowed his eyes.

He said, "Uh...I think we're having dinner with Logan and Taylor tomorrow night."

From the press of Mark's lips, he knew that was a lie, but I had no doubt that we'd be having dinner with them now. Either that or Logan would want to come and harass Cass. She'd been a bitch to me, on more than a handful of times, and he hadn't gotten over his dislike for her. "And speaking of Logan," Mason stood up. "We should go and make sure he's not doing anything that will land him in jail right now."

I stood as well. Looking at Analise, I nodded to her. "Congratulations again."

"Thank you, Samantha."

James nodded to us. I started to pick up my plate, but Malinda said, "Oh phewy on that. Leave it, Sam. I'm going to make Mark help with dishes. He doesn't know it, but we're going to have an in-depth conversation about this girlfriend of his."

"Oh great." He groaned.

She ignored him. "We'll see you guys later tonight?"

Mason nodded. "Yeah. We're just going to our mom's house. Taylor's over there. We'll be back tonight."

"Good. See you two."

As we left, it was a weird feeling. I felt like I was running away from my mother and her announcement wasn't a surprise. It didn't do anything to change my life. Her and James had been together for four years now. They'd had their own tough times and endured it together. They'd been engaged for the last two years. The marriage part was coming. It had been a matter of time, but still, hearing it said out loud with a date and everything, it was final. My hand found Mason's as we grabbed our coats and stepped outside the door. He and Logan really would be my stepbrothers. Our family would be finalized.

He glanced down at me. "You okay?"

I shook my head, holding tight to his hand. "That wedding is going to be one big fucked-up ceremony. That's all I'm thinking right now."

He grunted, placing his arm around my shoulders. He pulled me close to him. "Well, think of it this way, now Logan will be happy. He really can call you sister now."

Yeah. That was one silver lining, but it wasn't the marriage announcement that was the problem. Analise was back and she was never leaving again. That was the real undertones of the dinner.

ANOTHER ALTERNATIVE THAT WAS CUT

I was running.

Breathe. Run. Two, three, four steps in a row. Breathe again. Five, six, seven. Breathe. *Pump your elbows. Go farther. Go faster.* I had to keep going. This was my escape. I had to go, as long as I could, as far as I could. I needed to go until I couldn't breathe anymore.

Run.

Keep going.

Run more. Run faster.

Keep going.

That's all I was thinking, over and over. It was on repeat in my mind as I sped down the wood-chipped paths behind Fallen Crest. It was beautiful. I was weaving through red pines, up a small hill that was more a mountain, and back down only to speed up another hill/mountain. To the right of me was a deep valley. I got glimpses of it as the trees thinned, but I kept going. I'd stop at the very top of the last hill and watch the sunset. Then, I'd start back home. I'd get there just as the last of the sunlight would fade.

This was my pattern and I loved it. I felt exhilarated. I'd been running this path for the last week since Mason and I returned to Fallen Crest. So much had changed. Logan wasn't with us, which felt wrong. It was like an arm was missing, but he was staying with Taylor for the first half of the summer, remaining at Cain. Mason was home. He was working an internship at James' company for the first half of the summer. The second half would be in Cain. He'd leave for early football training. He didn't need to play. He could've gone pro after his sophomore year, but he wanted to finish out his years. He wanted to graduate with a degree. Being a football star at Cain University, and also one featured heavily on ESPN, he had to be 'good and saintly' off the field. I could tell it was hard on him, but he was home for the next month and a half and I knew he was more relaxed. There was less of a spotlight on him.

I did not hold the same sentiment.

Being home was not relaxing for me. Analise was back, had been for the last year and a half. We were fast approaching June. She moved back to Fallen Crest, leaving the group home where she'd been for almost two years. She returned the Christmas of our freshman year and I spent the next year and a half avoiding Fallen Crest as much as possible. I couldn't any longer.

Mason was here. So was I.

That's how we were. Where he went, I went. Where I went, so did he. We were together and everything had been 'quiet' since my freshman year, his sophomore year. No one tried breaking us up. No one tried hurting me, or hurting him. There'd been no 'fights' against an adversary. It'd been us, college, and stability. I loved it.

This summer was the end of peace. I could feel it in my bones, and it was part of the reason I'd been running two hours every night.

I was cresting to the top of the last hill now. My lungs were screaming, but I loved that feeling. They wanted a break. Too bad. I kept going, until every organ was yelling at me to stop. Once I got there, the last few steps until the entire town of Fallen Crest opened beneath me, I gave in and appeased my body. Stopping, my hands on my hips, I gulped in breaths.

It was beautiful. Nestled among trees and in a valley, this town had brought so much tragedy to my life, but it brought so much love as well.

Mason. Logan.

Heather.

Malinda and David.

Even Mark.

I was content. I had the family that I lost. Even a little sister, from my biological father who was now in my life again.

The only one missing was my actual mother, but she was waiting. I found the Kade mansion. It stuck out among all the other larger mansions in Fallen Crest. It was the largest. It was more a mausoleum. I remembered the first day Analise and I moved in. Things had been so different back then.

Things weren't like that anymore.

I had family. My eyes trailed to the house down the street and across from the Kade Mansion. Malinda and David lived there, the man who raised me all my life. He wasn't my birth father, but he was my father in every other way. And across from them was the house that Mason and Logan's mother bought. She wasn't there. She lived in Fallen Crest for Logan's last year of high school, but since he went to university, she had resumed her traveling lifestyle. She'd been in Paris, a favorite of hers, and was staying there for the last six months. Malinda and David had a room for me. Their house had become my 'home', but I was staying at Helen's house with Mason. It felt more like our house since it was just the two of us, and the last week had been glorious. It was like our own honeymoon. No Logan. No Nate. I loved both of them, but they lived with us at Cain University. Logan was Mason's brother. He was family. Nate was family too, Mason's best friend and Logan's bar buddy, but it was still nice to have the house to ourselves. No stepmother. No dad. Mark wasn't there. He was staying at his college for the summer as well. Just Mason and me, but even as I was thinking that, my eyes kept trailing back to the Kade Mansion.

She was there.

She being my mother. She hadn't said much over the last year and a half. There were a few phone calls, requests to go for coffee, or dinner. Or the two times James came to Cain and all of us went for dinner. I'd been able to push her to the farthest region of my mind, but she was there. I felt her. I felt her silent begging like a plaque. She wouldn't go away. I didn't think she ever would go away.

Analise wanted a relationship with me.

But, feeling the old panic that always rose up in me as I let myself think about it, my hands turned into fists and I couldn't let her in. My chest tightened. A wave of dizziness was threatening to crash over me.

I couldn't.

There was no way.

And, still feeling her on my back, as if she were physically standing behind me, I turned and started the run back home. This time, I felt as if I were being chased. She was with me, right behind me, always watching me.

I ran harder, kicking off with more force, but the run back wasn't as freeing as it had been before.

AN ALTERNATIVE BEGINNING TO FALLEN CREST PUBLIC

(This was deleted and a new storyline was created.)

CHAPTER ONE

When I let myself into Garrett's new house, I dropped my two bags in the foyer and walked to the kitchen. It was a large room with granite countertops and a steel-encased grill in the middle of it all. As I glanced around and skimmed where his office was, I knew I didn't need to look further. He wasn't there. And then I saw a note left on the counter and grabbed it.

'Heya, Sammy. Had to fly to Boston. Be back in deuces. Mi casa es su casa and I mean that. There's a tub of condoms in your bathroom. Tell your mom. I live to piss her off. C ya in dos dias, peaches!

G'

The note fluttered down as I let go of it and turned to survey the house. When my bio dad had decided to move closer and get to know me, no one had known how literally he meant it. He moved two houses down from James Kade's house. And when he gave me a key, extended his wish that I'd stay with him every now and then, Analise had flipped a lid. Plates had been shattered. Mugs were thrown across the room. She kicked a few vases over. When she had picked up a wine glass, she hesitated and set it back down. As she had done that, Mason and Logan both bent over in laughter.

James stood in the back and waited. It seemed like he was always waiting, but when my mom started to quiet down, he scooped her up in his arms and whisked her from the room. I didn't hear a word from my mother for three days after that and whatever James had been telling her, it must've worked. A week later my mom returned to her tea drinking, dress wearing, and being fake in ways that she'd taken up when we moved into the Kade mansion.

Analise Summers Strattan was back. Or—well—she was going to be Analise Summers Kade by the end of the summer. There'd been a hurry order placed on the divorce hearings and she was excited when she exclaimed the divorce would be final around Valentine's Day. My mother had been gleeful when she declared that was ironic timing.

My hate returned for her at that moment. But she didn't care. She turned back to the television with her wine and then her phone started lighting up. I heard enough to know that she was planning some benefit or banquet event.

I didn't care.

It wasn't long before Garrett had extended his first home welcoming. Everyone had gone, David included, but Analise stayed home. James went in her place. And I promised Garrett that Friday night to stay with him for an entire week the next Monday. It was that day today and when I returned home from school to pack, Analise spoke her first genuine words to me in nearly a month.

"Are you sure you have to go? I don't think it's safe. He flies back to Boston all the time. His firm is still there. What if he's not there? I don't want you to be alone. Sam, it's not safe. Don't go. Stay here. You can stay with him another time when we know he'll be there for sure. I'm not comfortable with this."

It went on and on like that. It was on the tip of my tongue to remind her that I wouldn't be alone, but that wasn't a conversation I wanted to remind her about. She disapproved of my relationship with Mason and I knew she would always disapprove. James hadn't liked it either. There'd been a few tense conversations between father and son, but Mason never shared what was said. He always shrugged and commented that James needed to say what he needed to say and then he would forget for awhile. And that'd been the pattern for the last three months.

When I had finally left the mansion and got into my car, I let out a deep breath of relief. I loved my mother. I loved my father, David. And

I even loved living with Mason and Logan, but I was excited to live in a house all by myself. Garrett would be there, I had no doubt, but like Analise had said—a part of me was okay if he wasn't. Peace. That's what I wanted. My life had been too dramatic for too long now.

But then I got inside, read the note, and a sense of disappointment filled me.

I really was alone and when I glanced at the clock, I knew it'd be hours until Mason would show up.

It was five now. I had four hours to kill.

And then I was doing something before I really knew what I was doing. I had my cellphone out and I had already pushed her number before I blinked at what was going on. Then I blinked and I held my breath.

When Becky answered, my heart skipped a beat and my fingers got clumsy. The phone fell from my hand and I yelled as I bent to scoop it up, "Don't hang up! Please. I dropped the phone. I'm coming back. I got it—" I panted as I plastered my phone against my ear. "Hey! Hi! How are you?"

There was silence on the other end.

I frowned, but rushed out, "You picked up. I'm hoping that's a good thing. Can you talk to me? I was really hoping you'd talk to me?"

Then I stopped and the silence grew painful. My heart beat in my ear and I gritted my teeth, but then she replied in a quiet voice, "Why are you calling me?"

"Uh, because I miss you. You haven't talked to me for three months, since…" I clasped my eyes shut. "I'm just happy that you answered! Thank you. Thank you for that."

There was some more silence again.

Then she murmured, "You don't ever call me, Sam. You were calling. Is something wrong?"

"No." I glanced around at the empty house. "Well, I mean, not really. I mean…"

"What's going on?"

"You see, my bio dad moved here. Did you know that?"

She seemed in pain as she admitted, "I might've heard that, yes."

"Okay, well, and I told him I'd stay with him for a week and today is the first day, but he's not here. He had to fly back to Boston so I'm all alone and this is a really big place and he has a theatre in the basement. It's pretty great, actually. I was thinking we could order a pizza, maybe have some wine even? I know he's got a bunch in one of these rooms, but I don't feel like exploring on my own and…" My heart was pounding now. "I don't know who else to call. Do you want to come over?"

"Why don't you call Mason or Logan?" She sounded so small.

I shrugged. "I don't know. It wouldn't be fun with them." And they had things to do after school, like their first basketball practice.

"Oh."

"So will you come?" I kept my eyes closed and waited.

"It's the new house next to the Kades, right?"

Why wasn't I surprised she had known that? I gripped the phone tighter and grinned into it. "Yes, that one. My car's in the driveway. It has the red gate."

"I know! I'll be there quick." And she hung up, sounding in a breathless excitement like I'd known her to be so many other times.

I shook my head as I let loose a deep breath. The girl was going to kill me. She'd become a friend when no one else wanted anything to do with me, but she found out three months ago that her fairytale hero had been using her to get to me and Becky ceased to exist from my life. The rumors hit not long after that about Mason and me and nothing seemed like normal anymore. I had people trying to be friends when they'd been the ones gossiping behind my back and others who decided they wanted to kill me when they had gotten along with me prior.

It didn't take that long until my doorbell rung. I had taken my bags to my room, ordered a pizza, and worried if I'd given the right address before I opened the door to Becky. She looked up and gave me a small smile. Her red hair was pulled back in two pigtails that were low on her head and she had her hands clasped together.

"Hi."

I grinned. I was just glad she'd shown up. "Hey." And I opened the door wider. "Come in. Please. I need company."

She grinned, but shook her head as she went in and her head started to swivel around. "This place is gorgeous, Sam. I can't believe it."

"Well," I felt so awkward. "My bio dad is a senior partner in his law firm so I guess…" I spread my arms wide. "That means he can own something like this."

She went from one room to the next. She started in the main living room with leather couches and a chandelier from the ceiling, to the next living room that had red couches. A piano had been placed in an open area by a small fountain and then she bypassed it the dining room and patio room. Both were extensions from the kitchen.

She arched an eyebrow. "Is this place bigger than the Kade mansion?"

"No." I cringed. I'd spoken too soon.

"Really?" Her awestruck tone had come back.

"I mean, that place is so formal and all."

"Is it bigger or not?" She pinned me down with her eyes.

I squirmed under her gaze and then relinquished, "No, it's not, but it's more modern. James' place is just huge."

She glanced under her eyelids at me before she looked away. "I wouldn't know. You never invited me over."

And this was where I held my tongue. I only knew one other person that'd been invited inside and I wasn't going to start any drama, had enough of that, so I never invited Becky over. It was something that I knew had hurt her, but I gave her a small smile instead of the response that she hadn't made the short list allowed inside. That conversation wouldn't end well.

"So you said you had a theatre here?"

"I did!" I perked up as I led her downstairs to the room with a screen that took up an entire wall. A few rows of lounging chairs made up the rest of it. Each chair could be reclined and they had a resting place for drinks and anything else someone might've brought.

"Oh my god!" Becky gasped as she walked inside. "This is amazing, Sam. Your bio dad thought about this, all on his own?"

I shrugged again. "He's one of a kind, trust me." When she lifted up a barrier between two of the seats, I started laughing. "Yeah, I liked the ideas of couches more, but then Mason showed me that. I like this room a lot more now."

Her smile faded quickly and I paused in confusion, but then I realized. We'd never talked about him before, but this was time and I took a deep breath. "You can ask anything you want, you know."

She let the barrier fall and turned back. The gravity in her eyes set me back, but I clenched my jaw and waited. She had a right to know, didn't she? She'd been my friend when I hadn't any so I owed her. Right? Pain seared me when I remembered two other friends that I would've thought the same, until both of them stabbed me in the back.

"How?"

She threw me with that one. "What do you mean?"

"How did it happen? Do you love him?"

I smiled weakly. "Maybe we could have some wine before we have this talk?"

She blocked me when I started for the door. "I mean it, Sam. I want to know. Are you really with him?" Then she blushed and looked down. "Of course, you are. I was there. I saw how he touched you. But…" She looked back up. "Why didn't you tell me?"

"I…" had no idea what to say to her. How could I explain things I didn't know myself? When I started to feel for him, when his touch excited me, when I knew I shouldn't have experienced the rush of adrenalin that I did? So I settled with, "It just happened, I guess. I don't really know—there wasn't an exact time when it happened."

"When we were at the cabin party, you were gone that first whole day. Was it then?"

Oxygen left me in a rush. "Okay, maybe that's when it started." A flash of lust spread through me as I remembered that day. His arms had held me in place as he nuzzled under my neck, to my cheeks, to my ear. Adam had been there and he'd been a witness to the power Mason held over me. Heat flared through me as I recalled that time. It wasn't one that I was proud of, but it pushed Adam back. I knew now that Mason had purposely paraded our relationship in front of the others for a reason.

"You were with him that day?"

I nodded.

Her cheeks flushed up and she squeezed her hands together, but she asked in a dreadful tone, "You had sex with him that day?"

Okay, enough with the sharing. I narrowed my eyes and asked in a flat voice, "Why do you care about that?"

She squeaked again and looked away. There was a frantic feeling to her when she hurried out, "I don't. I just—did you? I mean, Adam said you did and I didn't believe him."

It took one step before I latched onto her arm.

Her eyes were round as she gaped up at me.

I gritted my teeth and tried to contain my anger. It was like whiplash. "Are you kidding me? You would never care before. You would've been excited. Now you care? Now you're telling me Adam had something to say about it?"

She gulped and moved away from me. My hold tightened on her and her eyes got bigger when she tried to pull her arm from me. "Let go of me."

My eyes bore into her. I needed to know. "When it came out that Mason and I are dating and that Adam had been using you to get to me, you stopped talking to me. I thought it was because you felt hurt or betrayed, but now I'm starting to wonder. Why'd you stop talking to me, Becky?"

Her mouth had fallen open and she closed it now. Her eyes slid to the side.

"Tell me the truth too."

"I…" She took a deep breath. "IstoppedbecauseAdamwasmaking meconfused." Another deep breath. "Hesaidyouliedtomeonpurpose anddidn'tconsiderme," another breath. "afriendotherwiseyouwould've toldmeyouweredatingMasonKade,butnothatIblameyouwithJessica andLydiaandallthatcrap."

My fingers let loose and I was ashamed to see there were white finger prints on her arm. "You're an idiot, right? You know that, don't you?"

She gulped and hung her head. "I'm starting to think that."

"I didn't tell you about Mason because I don't trust anyone. You can't blame me for that. I caught Jeff cheating on me; then found out that Jessica had been screwing him for two years. Then, to make it worse, Lydia knew about it. My other best friend covered for them. And then you show up and we're friends for two months before this shit's hit the fan again. Can you blame me for not telling you?"

She gave me a sad look.

I narrowed my eyes and clipped out, "And Adam's talking to you? You're listening to the guy that used you because you were the only one I was talking to? Really? Come on, Becky. I know you think Adam Quinn is this great guy, but he can be really low and dirty if he doesn't get what he wants."

"I know." It came out like a whimper.

"Do you?"

Then the doorbell rang again and I let loose with a string of curses. "It's the pizza. Hold on."

For more free reads and extras, head to:
www.tijansbooks.com
Join her reader group: www.facebook.com/groups/tijansfanpage

Printed in Great Britain
by Amazon